Eating Isn't Always Easy

Ben's story
about his
Eosinophilic
Esophagitis

Nancy S. Rotter, Ph.D.

Qian Yuan, M.D., Ph.D.

Illustrated by Phoebe Rotter

ISBN: 1466440732
ISBN 13: 9781466440739
Library of Congress Control Number: 2011918995
CreateSpace, North Charleston, SC

This book is dedicated to children
with eosinophilic gastrointestinal disorders
and to their families

Acknowledgments

We would like to acknowledge the Demarest Lloyd, Jr. Foundation for their generous financial support and our colleagues at the Food Allergy Center of Massachusetts General Hospital for intellectual support and inspiration.

Introduction for Parents and Caregivers

Children who have eosinophilic esophagitis (EoE) or other eosinophilic gastrointestinal conditions are faced with many challenges. In addition to coping with the clinical symptoms, the diagnostic process, and the treatment of EoE, the emotional impact on the child and family can be significant.

This book was created to help children in preschool through early elementary school learn about the challenges associated with the diagnosis and treatment of EoE, with a focus on dietary treatment. The aim of the book is to help children who have EoE or other eosinophilic gastrointestinal disorders gain a better understanding of what they might experience during the treatment process, and how the condition can affect their feelings and daily lives. Our hope is that by reading this book, children with EoE will feel that there are other children who have similar experiences and that they will learn some new ways to cope with their condition.

The story describes the challenges Ben faces in the treatment of EoE. It focuses on the reaction that he has to his dietary restrictions, including feelings of anger and sadness. It also addresses the way Ben adapts to his new diet and discovers that he can do all of the things that he likes to do despite his restricted diet. In the story, Ben and his doctor work together as detectives to help solve the "mystery" of which foods are triggering his EoE so that Ben learns what he needs to do in order to keep himself healthy.

The book was written so that parents or caregivers could read it with their child. Although the book was written about a child with EoE, we hope that you will adapt the story as you read it to your child so that it applies to his or her particular eosinophilic gastrointestinal condition.

Thank you,

Qian Yuan, M.D., Ph.D.
Pediatric gastroenterologist

Nancy Rotter, Ph.D.
Pediatric psychologist

I'm Ben.

This is my house.
This is my family.

2

I love playing with my train set and drawing pictures.

I have a bike, and I just learned to ride it without training wheels. See, no training wheels!

I felt scared when I first started to ride without training wheels, but after I practiced a lot, it got easier and easier. I still feel a little scared when I fall off sometimes, but it always helps to get back on.

7

I have something called eosinophilic esophagitis. It's called EoE for short. It's a problem with the part of the body called the gastrointestinal system or GI system, which is where the food goes after you eat.

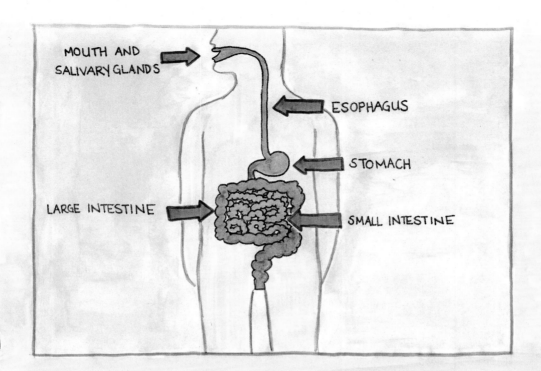

MOUTH AND SALIVARY GLANDS

ESOPHAGUS

STOMACH

LARGE INTESTINE

SMALL INTESTINE

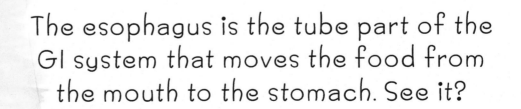

The esophagus is the tube part of the GI system that moves the food from the mouth to the stomach. See it?

When I was little, I used to get lots of tummy aches. Sometimes my throat hurt or I would gag and cough when I ate. I used to throw up a lot.

I didn't like eating very much.

My parents knew that something was wrong. They took me to see lots of nice doctors so they could figure out what was happening inside me. I had to have lots of medical tests. Some weren't so bad.

I was scared when I had to have
something called an endoscopy, or
"scope" for short. Before the test, I
was afraid of going to the hospital and
having sleepy medicine for the scope.

It turned out that it wasn't as scary as I thought it would be, just like riding my bike without training wheels turned out to be.

The scope helped the doctors figure out that I have EoE. The doctors told us that the reason I felt sick and had trouble eating was because of the EoE. They also told us that it was probably one or more foods I was eating that was causing the problem. The only way to figure out what foods were making me sick was for me to go on a special diet.

My GI doctor, or tummy doctor, told me that we were going to be detectives. We were going to solve the mystery of which foods might be causing the EoE. She told me that we would do this very carefully.

I would start by eating just a few foods. Then I would slowly add foods back into my diet. We would look for clues along the way to discover which foods were OK for my body and which ones made the EoE worse.

The first step in solving my EoE mystery was to have a lot of a special drink. My doctor told me that the drink would help me get all of the stuff my body needs to be healthy. She also said that it would help me feel better. I tasted three different kinds of special drinks: Elecare, Neocate, and Splash. Even though I chose Splash, it took me a little while to get used to the taste of it. I also got to eat a little bit of fruit.

After I started drinking Splash, I began to feel better. But I didn't like not being able to eat the things my sister got to have. The first step in solving the mystery sure was hard!

After I was on my diet awhile, I had another endoscopy, since it was the only way to tell for sure if I was getting better.

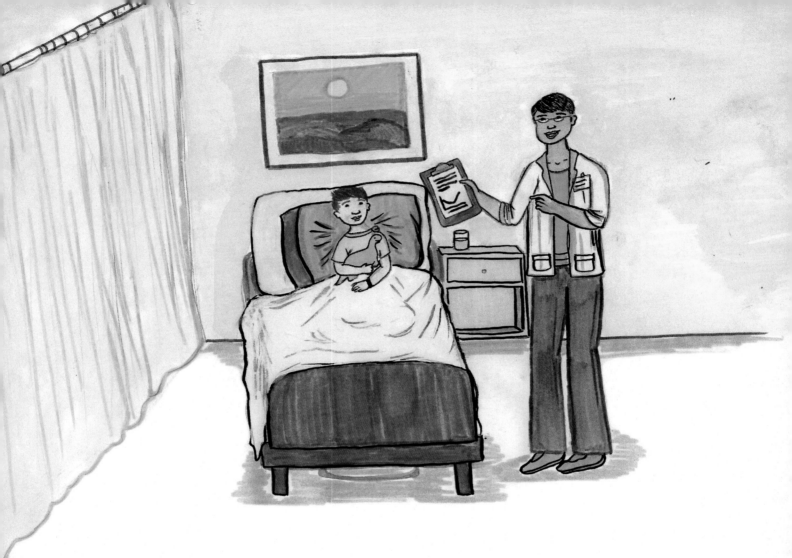

I wasn't as scared this time. The endoscopy showed that my esophagus was better. My GI doctor told me that I was doing an excellent job of being a detective. I got to add some more foods to my diet!

I had to go back to have scopes and see my GI doctor each time I added foods back into my diet. When my scopes looked good, I got to have even more foods back.

When the endoscopies showed the EoE was a problem again, it was a clue that the food I was eating was making my EoE worse. Usually, my body gave me clues before the scope: my throat hurt and I started throwing up again. When this happened, I had to stop eating that food, which made me sad. I did not like this part of being a detective.

SORBET

CUCUMBER

SMOOTHIES

GLUTEN-FREE PASTA

GLUTEN-FREE MUFFINS

CHICKEN

It took a LONG time, lots of scopes, and lots of visits to my doctor to solve the mystery of what was making my EoE worse. But with the help of my GI doctor and my good detective work, we were finally able to solve it!

The good news is that now I know what foods are healthy for me and what foods make the EoE get worse.

My body feels better when I eat the
foods that are healthy for me.

The not-so-good news is that dairy (things like milk, cheese, and ice cream) and wheat (like bread and pasta) make my EoE worse. I can't eat these anymore, which still makes me sad and mad sometimes.

We don't have many of these foods at my house, so it doesn't bother me too much when I eat with my family. Also, my parents have found some foods I can eat, like spaghetti made without wheat, and sorbet, which is like ice cream without milk.

It's still hard to go to friends' houses and birthday parties sometimes. I can't eat pizza, cake, or ice cream like my friends. But my parents have found some treats I can eat, so I bring them with me.

It helps that some of my friends are on special diets too. My neighbor, Sally, has a peanut allergy, so she can't have anything that might have peanuts in it. My best friend, Will, has something called Celiac disease, so he can't eat wheat, like me.

It's nice to know that I'm not the only one who
has to be careful about what I'm eating.

Even though I can't eat the same things that my friends and family can eat I can still do all of the things that I like to do. I can ride my bike. I can draw pictures. I can play with my trains.

And I can be a good detective.

Resources for Families

American Partnership for Eosinophilic
Disorders (APFED)
PO Box 29545
Atlanta, GA 30359
Phone: (713) 493-7749
www.apfed.org

Food Allergy and Anaphylaxis Network
(FAAN)
11781 Lee Jackson Hwy., Suite 160
Fairfax, VA 22033-3309
Phone: (800) 929-4040
www.foodallergy.org

American Gastroenterology Association
(AGA)
4930 Del Ray Avenue
Bethesda, MD 20814
Phone: (301) 654-2055
www.gastro.org

North American Society for Pediatric
Gastroenterology, Hepatology and
Nutrition (NASPGHAN)
PO Box 6
Flourtown, PA 19031
Phone: (215) 233-0808
www.naspghan.org

Eosinophilic Gastrointestinal Disease
Support Group of Boston (EGID)
Boston, MA
www.egidboston.org

About the Authors

Nancy S. Rotter, PhD. is a licensed pediatric psychologist with over twenty years of clinical experience. She is a senior staff psychologist at Massachusetts General Hospital and an assistant clinical professor in child psychiatry at Harvard Medical School. Dr. Rotter works in the Food Allergy Center at Massachusetts General Hospital, where she collaborates with allergists, gastroenterologists, and nutritionists in the treatment of children who have food allergies and eosinophilic gastrointestinal conditions. She provides children and their parents with support and coping techniques to help manage children's medical conditions and the associated stress of these illnesses. Dr. Rotter frequently speaks to parent groups about helping children who have food allergies and eosinophilic conditions. She is particularly interested in the relationship between anxiety and medical illness in children. Dr. Rotter also has a private practice in Newton, Massachusetts, where she specializes in the cognitive behavioral treatment of children with anxiety. When she is not working, she enjoys gardening, antiquing, and creating art from the old things she collects. She lives in Boston, Massachusetts, with her family.

Qian Yuan, M.D., Ph.D. is the clinical director of the Food Allergy Center at Massachusetts General Hospital in Boston and is an assistant clinical professor in pediatrics at Harvard Medical School. He specializes in pediatric gastroenterology and nutrition. Dr. Yuan attended Beijing Second Medical College in Beijing, China, and received a PhD in immunology at the University of Auckland, New Zealand. He did pediatric residency and pediatric fellowship training in gastroenterology and nutrition at Massachusetts General Hospital and Children's Hospital Boston. Dr. Yuan's clinical focus is eosinophilic esophagitis and eosinophilic gastrointestinal diseases. He lives in Sharon, Massachusetts, with his wife and two daughters.

About the Illustrator

Phoebe Rotter is attending Kenyon College, where she majors in art history. This is her first time illustrating, and it has been an incredible experience. When Phoebe is not drawing, she likes to sing, dance, and explore the woods.

Made in the USA
Middletown, DE
02 December 2015